MINI CLASSICS
THE
SECRET
GARDEN

Retold by Stephanie Laslett
Illustrated by Robin Lawrie

SHOOTING STAR PRESS

TITLES IN SERIES I AND III OF THE MINI CLASSICS INCLUDE:

SERIES I

Aladdin and the Magic Lamp
Ali Baba and the Forty Thieves
Alice in Wonderland
A Child's Garden of Verses
Cinderella
The Emperor's New Clothes
The Frog Prince
Goldilocks and the Three Bears
Hansel and Grettel
The Happy Prince
The Little Mermaid
Mother Goose's Rhymes
The Owl and the Pussycat (and other Nonsense Verse)
Puss in Boots
Sleeping Beauty
Snow White and the Seven Dwarfs
The Town Mouse and the Country Mouse (and other
    Aesop's Fables)
The Three Little Pigs
The Ugly Duckling
The Wizard of Oz

Series III

© Parragon Book Service Ltd

This edition printed for:
Shooting Star Press, Inc.
230 Fifth Avenue-Suite 1212,
New York, NY 10001

Shooting Star Press books are available at special
discounts for bulk purchases for sales promotions,
premiums, fund-raising, or educational use. Special
editions or book excerpts can also be created to
specification. For details contact: Special Sales
Director, Shooting Star Press, Inc., 230 Fifth Avenue,
Suite 1212, New York, New York 10001.

ISBN 1-56924-243-7

Printed and bound in Great Britain.

Mary Lennox was thin and pale, with a grumpy face and a bad temper. She was born in India and because her father was so busy working and her mother was so occupied with her grand parties poor Mary was left alone for much of the time. She had no friends to play with and was brought up by an Indian nurse-maid, an Ayah, who did everything for her.

One day the Lennox's cook caught a dreadful disease. Everybody was terrified and many of the servants ran away.

Those that stayed behind at the house soon fell ill themselves and eventually all who remained had died, including Mary's parents. Mary was left completely alone, the only survivor.

When Mary was rescued from that dreadful plague it was decided that she should be sent to live with her uncle in England.

So it was that Mary found herself arriving at Misslethwaite Manor late one night as the cold mist swirled about her. She was met by the housekeeper, Mrs Medlock, a stout lady with red cheeks and sharp black eyes.

"My word! You're a plain little piece of goods!" remarked the woman, as she inspected Mary. "You certainly haven't inherited your mother's beauty."

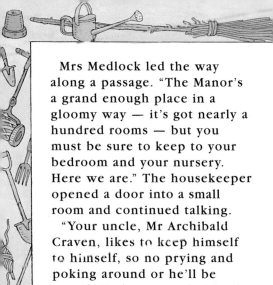

Mrs Medlock led the way along a passage. "The Manor's a grand enough place in a gloomy way — it's got nearly a hundred rooms — but you must be sure to keep to your bedroom and your nursery. Here we are." The housekeeper opened a door into a small room and continued talking.

"Your uncle, Mr Archibald Craven, likes to keep himself to himself, so no prying and poking around or he'll be vexed. He has a crooked back and that set him wrong right from the start. He was a sour

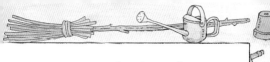

young man and got no pleasure from his money until he was married." Mary looked at Mrs Medlock in surprise. She hadn't known he had a wife.

"Ah, me," sighed Mrs Medlock, shaking her head. "His pretty young wife died some years ago. He loved her more than anything else on earth and since her death he's been odder than ever. He cares about nobody and won't let anyone see him apart from Pitcher, his manservant. So you be sure to keep out of his way, do you hear me?"

Mary climbed on the window-seat and stared out into the night, her lips pinched tightly together. The wind blew across the moor and the rain began to stream down the windowpane.

"I shall not want to go poking about," said sour little Mary, and her heart felt heavy as lead.

The next morning she woke
to the sound of a maidservant
noisily raking out the cinders
in the fireplace.

"Are you my servant?" asked
Mary, haughtily. The girl sat
back on her heels and laughed.

"My name's Martha Sowerby,"
she said. "But as I'm to do the
housemaid's work up here I'll
wait on you a bit, if you like."

"Then dress me, Martha,"
ordered Mary. "I cannot dress
myself."

"Then it's high time you
learned," replied the girl,
gaping in astonishment.

15

Martha held up a white dress.

"Here are your new clothes. Mr Craven sent them for he did not want a child in black wandering about the place," she explained and soon, with a bit of help doing the buttons, Mary had dressed herself for the first time in her life. As the little girl reluctantly picked at her porridge, Martha described her own family.

"There's twelve of us and my father only gets sixteen shillings a week to feed us all. My brothers and sisters play on the moor all day long and young Dickon even has his own wild pony. Animals just love Dickon, they do." Martha looked at Mary's pale, sickly face. "You could do with getting a bit of fresh air in your lungs," she decided. "Out you go and play," and soon Mary found herself outside in the rambling garden.

"There is one walled garden which you must not go into," warned Martha. "It was the master's wife's garden and when she died he locked the door and buried the key. No-one has been in it for ten years."

Slowly Mary walked down
the path and thought about
her uncle. She doubted she
would ever meet him and was
glad, for she felt sure he
would not like her. "People
never like me and I never like
people," she thought. Just then
a clear rippling sound broke
out and, turning round, Mary
saw a little robin in an apple
tree. The tree grew inside a
garden with a high wall all
around it and, try as she
might, Mary could find no
door to let her inside and get
closer to the friendly robin.

He had such a cheerful song that it brought a look into her sour little face that was almost a smile. He flew off over the wall and Mary followed him into the kitchen garden. There she found an old man digging with a spade. He had a surly, unfriendly face, but when he caught sight of the robin he broke into a slow smile. Mary thought how much nicer a person looked when he smiled. She had not thought of it before.

"I reckon he's lonely," said the gardener. "He wants company." Mary thought for a while.

"I'm lonely, too," she said in a whisper, and realised that this was one of the things that made her feel sour and cross. "He lives in the walled garden, but I can't find the door." To Mary's surprise, the gardener's smile faded in an instant. "Don't tha go poking tha nose around there," he replied with a scowl. Then he picked up his spade and stomped off.

At first each day passed by exactly like the others. She had nothing and nobody to play with and so spent her time outdoors, running against the wind.

Little by little the good fresh
air brought colour to her cheeks
and an appetite to her stomach
and soon she found she was
able to eat all her porridge
each morning and so she grew
stronger and healthier with
each passing day.

One place she went to again
and again was the strange
walled garden without a door.
She was very curious to know
more about it and one evening
as she sat on the rug before
the fire she asked Martha why
Mr Craven had locked the door
and buried the key.

Martha looked unsure of whether she should answer.

"Well, his pretty wife spent all her time there," she said quietly. "She tended it herself and made a little rose bower over the branch of a tree which dipped down and was like a seat for her. One day the branch broke and she was hurt so bad she died. And then the doctor thought Mr Craven would die, too, for he was so upset. That's why he hates that garden and that's why no-one has been in it since."

Mary felt a new feeling. She

felt sorry for poor Mr Craven.

Just then she heard a sound, half muffled by the wind.

"Did you hear someone crying?" she asked Martha. Martha looked startled and shook her head violently. Just then a great draught came rushing along the passage and the nursery door blew open with a crash. Then the cry could be plainly heard — a child's cry!

"It must have been the wind," insisted Martha, but something in her manner made Mary sure she was not telling the truth.

One rainy day Mary decided she would explore the house. Her corridor branched into other corridors and led her deeper and deeper into the house. Her footsteps echoed down the long empty passages and it seemed as if there was no-one else but her in the whole of Misslethwaite Manor.

As she wandered further and
further from her own rooms,
she realised she was lost. She
stopped near a tapestry door
to try and get her bearings and
in the still quiet heard the
unmistakable sound of a child
sobbing. Mary turned towards
the door with a beating heart
but was terrified to see Mrs
Medlock bearing down on her.

"What are you doing here?"
she demanded, grabbing the
little girl's arm. "I'm sure I
heard someone crying,"
quavered Mary, but the housekeeper shushed her crossly.

"You heard nothing of the kind," she retorted. "Back to your room and no more nonsense."

Alone again, Mary stamped her foot. "There *was* someone crying!" she said. "There was!"

Two days later the weather dawned bright and clear for the first time since Mary arrived at the Manor. She had never seen such a beautiful blue sky and out in the garden the little robin was in full song. How happy Mary was when he hopped right up close to her. "At last I have a friend," she thought as she watched him pecking in the rich earth.

31

Suddenly she looked closely at
the bare flower bed. The robin
hopped over the freshly turned
mounds of soil and Mary caught
a glimpse of something shining.
Bending down, she brushed the
earth away and found she was
looking at a rust-spotted old key.

"Perhaps this is the key to the
garden!" she whispered.

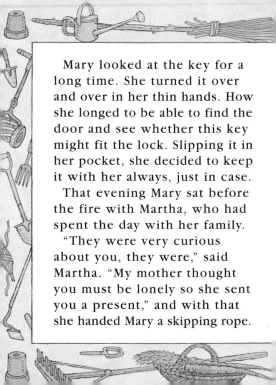

Mary looked at the key for a long time. She turned it over and over in her thin hands. How she longed to be able to find the door and see whether this key might fit the lock. Slipping it in her pocket, she decided to keep it with her always, just in case.

That evening Mary sat before the fire with Martha, who had spent the day with her family.

"They were very curious about you, they were," said Martha. "My mother thought you must be lonely so she sent you a present," and with that she handed Mary a skipping rope.

"What is it for?" asked Mary, curiously. So the next day Martha taught her how to skip and soon they were both pink-cheeked and laughing. Mary was eager to try her skipping rope outdoors and as she skipped into the kitchen garden, old Ben Weatherstaff lifted his head in astonishment.

"Well, p'raps tha's got child's blood in tha veins instead of sour buttermilk after all," he said. Mary was halfway down the long path alongside the garden wall when she stopped to catch her breath. High on the wall was the robin and he greeted her with a chirp.

Just then a gust of wind rushed down the walk and swung aside the loose ivy trails overhanging the wall. Mary gasped. She had seen something. Pulling aside the ivy, she saw the thing she thought she would never find — the door to the secret garden.

With her heart in her mouth, she pulled out the rusty key and found it fitted the keyhole. Then she turned it in the lock and the door slowly opened. With a quick look to make sure no-one was coming, she pushed back the curtain of ivy and slipped inside.

37

It was a strange and lovely place. The high walls were covered with the bare stems of climbing roses and their branches reached out from tree to tree in a hazy tangle and made mysterious bridges, swinging with long trailing tendrils.

"How still it is!" whispered Mary. "And I am the first person to speak in here for ten years." Even the robin remained motionless as he watched Mary explore the forgotten garden. She thought that maybe all the plants were dead, but suddenly saw some tiny green shoots in a flowerbed.

"It isn't quite a dead garden," she cried and she began to clear the weeds and grass away from the pale green points so that they could breathe more easily. So she went from bed to bed and two hours flew by. When the courtyard bell struck midday, Mary slipped out of the door and ran back for her dinner.

"I wish I could have a little spade," she told Martha.

"What for?" asked Martha. Mary thought hard. She must be sure not to reveal her secret.

"I would love to plant some seeds of my own and watch them

grow, like Ben Weatherstaff
does," she replied.

"Well, now! What a good idea,"
approved Martha. "And I know
just the person to help you choose
your seeds. You write a letter to
our Dickon and he'll pick the best
ones for you at the village shop."

And so Mary set to work and
before long the envelope and
money had been sent off to
Mrs Sowerby's cottage.

All week the sun shone down
and every day Mary went to the
secret garden. She liked the
feeling that when its beautiful
old walls shut her in, no-one

knew where she was. It seemed to her like something out of a fairy tale.

Mary was an odd, determined little person and now she had something interesting to do, she was completely lost in her work. She pulled up weeds and found many more shoots than she could ever have imagined possible. She was always careful to dart in and out of the garden when no-one was about and many a time she gave Ben Weatherstaff a turn by suddenly appearing at his side.

"Th'art like the robin," he said.

"I never know when I'll see thee or where tha's sprung from!"

One day as Mary ran down the path to her garden she heard a strange whistle. The sound led her to an old garden shed and round the back, sitting on an old tree trunk, she found a boy playing a wooden pipe. He had a turned-up nose and cheeks as red as poppies and the bluest eyes imaginable. Watching him were a squirrel and two rabbits and when he saw Mary he stood up slowly and smiled.

"I'm Dickon," he said. "I know that you are Miss Mary."

Mary knew nothing about boys and felt quite stiff and shy.

"I've got your garden tools and seeds," said Dickon, and soon Mary had quite forgotten her shyness as they poured over the seed packets together.

"These are white poppy, and these are larkspur," he explained. "Tell you what. I'll help you plant them, if you like. Where's your garden?" Mary froze and her thin hands clutched her skirt. Dickon noticed she was upset and he was puzzled.

"Won't they give you a bit of garden?" he asked gently.

Mary turned to look at him. Could she trust this boy? With a deep breath she began to speak.

"Can you keep a secret, if I tell you one? But you mustn't tell anyone or I should simply die!"

"Why, I keep the animals' secrets all the time," replied Dickon softly.

"Well...I've stolen a garden!" said Mary quickly. "Nobody wants it, nobody cares for it except me and they're letting it die, all shut in by itself!"

Then Mary decided to let him see the garden for himself and soon they were both safe inside.

"Ee, it's like a dream," he said.

For two or three minutes he stood looking around him and then began to walk about softly.

"I never thought I'd see this place," he whispered as he ran his hand along a grey branch.

"Is everything dead?" asked Mary. "No, not all of them," replied the boy and he took out a pocket knife and cut through a brown shoot. "See here, there's green in that wood. That's alive." Then Dickon and Mary went round the garden and soon they were both hard at work. He cut away the dead wood whilst she used the fork and the hoe.

The boy was much impressed by what Mary had managed to do on her own. "You've cleared around the snowdrops and the crocuses — and these daffydown-dillys here!" he said. "But there's so much more to do."

"Will you help me, Dickon?" asked Mary. "Will you come again?"

"I'll come every day if you want me, rain or shine!" he replied. "But we shan't make it too tidy for it won't be like a secret garden if it's too spick and span."

Mary could hear the dinner bell ringing but she stopped and turned back at the door.

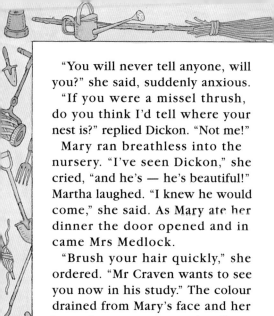

"You will never tell anyone, will you?" she said, suddenly anxious.

"If you were a missel thrush, do you think I'd tell where your nest is?" replied Dickon. "Not me!"

Mary ran breathless into the nursery. "I've seen Dickon," she cried, "and he's — he's beautiful!" Martha laughed. "I knew he would come," she said. As Mary ate her dinner the door opened and in came Mrs Medlock.

"Brush your hair quickly," she ordered. "Mr Craven wants to see you now in his study." The colour drained from Mary's face and her heart began to thump loudly.

She dreaded the thought of meeting her uncle but Mrs Medlock chivvied her along until she found herself in a part of the house she had never seen before and facing a man in an armchair. He had high crooked shoulders and black hair streaked with white. He would have been handsome had he not looked so miserable.

"I had forgotten all about you," he said slowly. "I was going to send you a nursemaid or a governess, but I forgot."

"I am too old for a nursemaid and please, please don't send me a governess," begged Mary.

The man looked at her in such a sad way that Mary could hardly talk. "I just want to run and skip and play outside. I won't do any harm," she said in a small voice.

"Don't look so worried," replied Mr Craven, sorrowfully. "You may do what you like. I have been a very poor guardian to you. Is there anything you need?"

"Might I," quavered Mary, "might I have a bit of earth?" The man looked at her and a strange, haunted look came into his eyes.

"You may take whatever bit of earth you want," he whispered, "and make it come alive."

When Mary returned to her nursery she jumped for joy. "I can have my garden!" she told Martha happily. "And Mr Craven seems really a nice man, but he looks so very sad."

Then she remembered she had left Dickon hard at work in the garden and, running through the little wooden door, she searched for him amongst the trailing roses. He was nowhere to be found but he had left a note on a tree. "I WILL CUM BAK" it said, and he had drawn a beautiful picture of a missel thrush sitting on her nest.

That night it rained heavily and Mary was awakened by the sound of the wind wuthering around the corners of the old house. Suddenly she sat up. She could hear another sound rising above the wind. It was the sound of someone crying.

"This time I will find out who it is," said Mary to herself and, picking up the candle, she tiptoed down the corridor. As she wandered in the gloom she could hear the crying getting nearer. Soon she was outside the tapestry door and she pushed it to one side.

Stepping through, she found
herself in a pitch-black corridor.
A glimmer of light came from
underneath one of the doors
and the crying was coming from
inside the room. Slowly Mary
pushed open the door and there
in the flickering shadows she
saw a boy lying on a huge four-
poster bed, lit by the soft glow
of a fire in the hearth. He had
a pale delicate face and large
grey eyes and as Mary stepped
inside the room, he looked up.

"Are you a ghost?" he said in
a frightened whisper.

"No," replied Mary. "Are you?"

The boy stared and stared at her with his huge eyes. At last he spoke again. "I am Colin Craven."

"I am Mary Lennox. Mr Craven is my uncle," said Mary.

"He is my father," said the boy.

"I didn't know he had a boy!" gasped Mary. "Why did nobody tell me?" "Because they knew I would not want you to see me," replied Colin. "I am always like this, ill in bed and I am sick of people staring at me and having my uncle, Dr Craven, talking over me. If I live I will most likely have a hunchback — but I won't live. My father hates to see me because my mother died when I was born and it makes him wretched to look at me."

"Do you never go out?" asked Mary. Colin shook his head.

"I hate the fresh air so I stay in bed all the time and everyone has to do as I ask. It makes me ill to be angry. How old are you?" he asked suddenly.

"I am ten, and so are you," said Mary. "You must be ten because when you were born the garden door was locked and the key was buried." Colin stared at her, bewildered, so Mary explained what his father had done.

"I could make the gardeners open it up," said Colin. "They would have to obey me. If I live, then Misslethwaite Manor shall be mine and I shall be master, but I don't suppose I shall live. I think Dr Craven wants me to die for then he will inherit the Manor."

"Do you want to live?" asked Mary.

"No," he replied irritably, "but I don't want to die. When I think about it I can't stop crying. But I don't want to talk about it. I want to talk about the garden. I am going to find out where the key is hidden and get them to open it up for me." His eyes shone

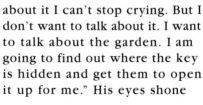

for the first time in years.

Mary's hands clutched each other and she sobbed out loud.

"Oh, don't — don't — don't do that!" she gasped. "If you do, it will never be a secret again! It would be so much better if we could maybe just — just find it ourselves and keep it our secret and perhaps we could find a strong boy who could push your wheelchair and we could go there without anybody knowing and it would be our secret and we wouldn't have to share it with anybody." She looked up at Colin with tears in her eyes.

Colin lay back on his pillow and a strange expression came over his face. "I should like that," he said, and as he dozed Mary described what she thought the

garden *might* be like.

"It might have rose trees in it," she whispered, "and maybe a little robin might live there."

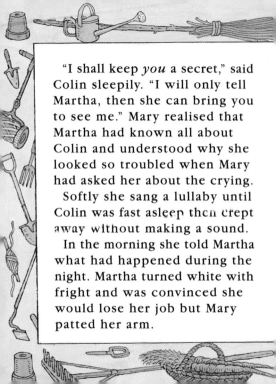

"I shall keep *you* a secret," said Colin sleepily. "I will only tell Martha, then she can bring you to see me." Mary realised that Martha had known all about Colin and understood why she looked so troubled when Mary had asked her about the crying.

Softly she sang a lullaby until Colin was fast asleep then crept away without making a sound.

In the morning she told Martha what had happened during the night. Martha turned white with fright and was convinced she would lose her job but Mary patted her arm.

"Don't worry! We are keeping it a secret. We spoke for a long time and I sang him to sleep."

Martha was astonished for she knew that the boy usually screamed and shouted if anyone tried to visit him.

"You must have bewitched him," she told Mary in complete wonderment. Just then the bell jangled and Martha hurried off to see who wanted her. She was back in five minutes with a strange expression on her face.

"It's young Master Colin. He wishes me to bring you to him," she said.

When Mary entered his room she was surprised to see him out of bed and sitting on a sofa, wrapped in a velvet dressing-gown.

"I've been thinking about you all morning," said Colin.

"I've been thinking about you, too," answered Mary.

Colin spoke to Martha in a grand manner and was so imperious that he reminded Mary of a young Rajah she had once seen in India. Secretly she thought him rather rude and spoiled but thought that if she could only get him out in the fresh air he might change, just as she felt she had done.

When they were alone, Mary began to talk once more about trees and flowers and soon she was describing Dickon.

"He knows all about foxes and badgers and all the plants that grow on the moor," she said.

"I hate the moor!" said Colin. "Such a great, bare, dreary place."

"It's beautiful!" protested Mary. "You should go there and see."

But Colin replied that he would never go anywhere because he was going to die. Mary grew quite impatient. "It's high time you decided you want to live and forget all this talk of dying," she cried. "You should meet Dickon. He never talks of death, only life and the living, and he has such blue eyes and such red cherry cheeks!" Mary's eyes sparkled as she remembered him.

She began to talk and talk
about Dickon's mother and old
Ben Weatherstaff and soon Colin
was laughing and then they
sounded for all the world like
two ordinary, healthy ten year
olds, instead of a hard, unloving
little girl and a sickly boy who
believed he was going to die.

They were laughing about the
robin when the door opened
and in walked Dr Craven and
Mrs Medlock. They stood
stockstill in the doorway,
mouths agape in astonishment.

"And what is the meaning of
this?" thundered the doctor.

Then Colin reminded Mary of the young Rajah once again.

"This is my cousin, Mary Lennox," he said calmly. "I like her and she must come and talk to me whenever I send for her."

Dr Craven looked angry and Mrs Medlock wrung her hands.

"I don't know what happened, sir," she said nervously. "None of the servants would dare talk."

"She heard me crying and came to find me," explained Colin.

Dr Craven felt his pulse. "You must be careful. Excitement is not good for you, my boy."

"Nonsense!" replied Colin. "She

has made me feel better and now I want her to have tea with me. Tell the nurse." The doctor did not dare forbid it but he looked most unhappy. As he walked down the corridor Mrs Medlock turned to him.

"He does look better, sir," she ventured, but the doctor did not reply.

The next week heavy rain stopped Mary from visiting her garden and so she spent a lot of time with Colin. She often wondered if she might trust him with her secret and whether or not he would like Dickon.

The next day dawned bright and clear. Mary *had* to see her garden. She couldn't wait! Quickly she ran outside and down the long path. Suddenly she stopped, for high on the wall perched a glossy black crow. It slowly flapped away as she ducked down through the door. There, to her surprise and delight, was Dickon and with him was a young fox cub with a bushy red tail.

"This is Captain," he explained, "and this here is Soot," and he pointed to the crow which had landed on his shoulder.

"When we smelt the air this morning we dashed over the moor, singing and cawing and barking — we just couldn't help it!" and he and Mary laughed aloud as they felt the spring working its magic all around them. Just then a red streak darted past them. It was the robin, busy nest building

"Dickon," whispered Mary. "I've met Colin." Dickon turned to look at her. "He wants me to visit him. I make him forget about dying," she said. The boy looked relieved. "I'm real happy to hear that," he said. "I had been told to keep quiet about him but it made me feel bad."

"He is strange," sighed Mary. "He keeps thinking he is going to die and it is so sad to see him shut away in the dark."

"He would stop thinking that if he came out and got some fresh air in his lungs," said Dickon. And so they agreed they would try and bring him outside. When Mary ran back for dinner, Martha met her with a long face. "Master Colin has been in a terrible temper," she said. "He has kept asking for you and is having a tantrum."

Mary ran to his room. "I've been with Dickon," she said.

"I will send him away if you do not come to me," scowled Colin.

"If you do, I will never come again," shouted Mary. "I will force you to!" cried Colin. Mary gasped. "You are the most selfish boy in the world." Colin bit his lip. "I'm ill," he said, "I'm dying." "No, you're not," replied Mary. "You just say that to make us feel sorry for you." Colin began to scream. "Stop it," shouted Mary. "I can scream as loud as you!" and to her surprise, Colin stopped and began to cry.

"I'm so unhappy," he sobbed.

Mary stood close beside him.
"You would be happier if you
came outside," she said. Then
she found herself telling him
all about the secret garden and
how she knew the way in.
Colin's eyes grew rounder and
rounder and a gleam of hope
crept into their grey depths

Some days later Mary brought
Dickon to meet Colin. He
arrived with Captain, Soot, his
two pet squirrels and a new-
born lamb and as they all
trooped into his room, Colin
was simply lost for words.

But Dickon was as friendly as if he had known Colin all his life and soon they were laughing together as they fed the lamb.

The next day the sun shone, the birds sang and Mary knew this was the day to take Colin to the secret garden. His eyes shone as Dickon pushed him out into the sunshine. Quickly they made their way to the little door and soon they were all three safe inside. Colin stared in wonderment at the rose trees and flowers and sunshine. "I *shall* get well!" he cried. "I shall live forever!"

It seemed as if that afternoon was the most perfect there had ever been and every hour the sunshine grew more golden. Colin watched as Mary and Dickon gardened

"Soon you'll be walking along with us," said Dickon.

"Walking! I'm too afraid to try for my legs are so thin and weak and shaky," sighed Colin.

"Well, when you've stopped being afraid, you will stand on them," said Dickon, but Colin wasn't listening. He was staring up at the wall.

"Who is that man?" he said.

Mary looked up in horror to see
Ben Weatherstaff glaring down
at her. "Tha young bad 'un!" he
shouted. "What's tha doing in
there?" Then his jaw dropped
as he caught sight of Colin.

"Why, it's Master Colin!"
cried Ben. "But — but thou art
a cripple and a hunchback."
Colin sat straight in his chair.

"I am *not* a cripple!" he cried.

"He's not!" cried Mary. Colin's
cheeks flamed red as he threw
the rugs off his lap. Clinging
to Dickon's arm, he slowly
pulled himself to his feet.

"Just look at me!" he cried.

Then Ben Weatherstaff gulped and suddenly the tears coursed down his wrinkled old cheeks.

"Eh! the lies some folks tell," he said. "Tha'll make a man yet, God bless tha!" It did his old heart good to see the children bringing the garden to life. And certainly its magic seemed to work wonders with Colin. As the weeks passed his legs grew stronger and soon he was able to walk slowly past the roses.

"What would Dr Craven say to see you now?" giggled Mary.

"He is not going to find out. I shall keep it a secret until I am

really well and then I shall walk
into my father's study and say
'I will grow to be a man'."

And so Ben kept the secret,
but some weeks later they
decided that Dickon's mother
could be trusted and one day
she was shown into the garden
and introduced to Colin. Her
blue eyes grew misty. "Eh,
dear lad," she said. "Thou art
so like tha' dear mother!"

Mrs Sowerby could not
believe the change in the boy
and decided it was high time
his father returned and saw
the difference for himself.

Mr Craven was travelling in Switzerland with only his memories for company. One day he fell asleep by the side of a lake and dreamt he heard his beloved wife calling his name. "Lilias!" he answered. "Where are you?" "I am in the garden!" the voice replied. When he awoke he felt at peace for the first time in years. The next morning a letter arrived for him from Yorkshire.

"Dear Sir," it said. "I would come home if I was you. I think your lady would ask you to. Yours faithfully, Susan Sowerby."

91

And so he returned to Misslethwaite Manor. Mrs Medlock
seemed flustered and said he
would find Colin outside.

As if in a dream, Mr Craven
slowly walked towards the
secret garden. Suddenly the
little wooden door burst open
and a fine tall boy ran out,
laughing merrily. He almost fell
into Mr Craven's arms, then
stopped and looked up at him
with his beautiful grey eyes.

"Colin! Is it you?" whispered
the man.

"Yes, father, it is I, and I am
going to live forever and ever!"

Then the boy drew him into the garden to meet Mary and Dickon. Mr Craven held his son's hand as if he would never let him go and as the warm sun slipped behind the green-gold of the trees, they walked back arm in arm towards the house — the Master of Misslethwaite and Colin, as strong and steady as any boy in Yorkshire!

FRANCES HODGSON BURNETT

Frances Hodgson Burnett wrote many books
for adults and children, but *The Secret
Garden* is by far her best loved story.
The idea came to her while she was planting
a new garden for herself. She remembered
the Rose Garden she had created many
years earlier at Maytham Hall, a beautiful
manor house in Kent and a former
home of hers. Some years after Mrs Burnett
left Maytham Hall she was most upset to
hear that the new owners had uprooted all
her rose bushes and turned it into a
vegetable garden. With this story she created
a garden that nobody would ever be able to
destroy, a garden that would live forever.